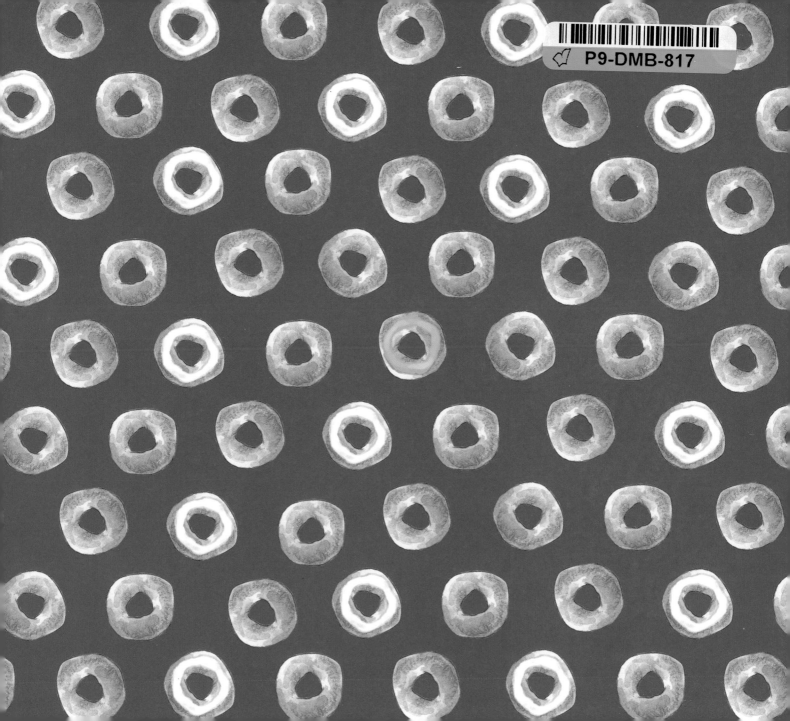

Hoogie in the Middle

Stephanie McLellan
& Dean Griffiths

pajamapress

Canada Council Conseil des Arts for the Arts du Canada    **ONTARIO ARTS COUNCIL CONSEIL DES ARTS DE L'ONTARIO**

The publisher gratefully acknowledges the support of the Canada Council for the Arts and the Ontario
Arts Council for its publishing program. We acknowledge the financial support of the Government of
Canada through the Canada Book Fund (CBF) for our publishing activities.

Library and Archives Canada Cataloguing in Publication

McLellan, Stephanie Simpson, 1959-
       Hoogie in the middle / Stephanie McLellan ; illustrated
by Dean Griffiths.
ISBN 978-1-927485-28-6
       I. Griffiths, Dean, 1967- II. Title.
PS8575.L457H66 2013   jC813'.6   C2012-906892-6

Publisher Cataloging-in-Publication Data (U.S.)

McLellan, Stephanie, 1959-
    Hoogie in the middle / Stephanie McLellan ; Dean Griffiths.
[32] p. : col. ill. ;   cm.
Summary: Pumpkin is big and smart and dependable. Tweezle is small and cute and loveable.
Hoogie feels like there is no room for a middle child until Mom and Dad remind her what a special
place the middle can be.
ISBN-13: 978-1-927485-28-6
1. Brothers and sisters – Juvenile fiction. 2. Middle-born children – Juvenile fiction. 3. Emotions in
children – Juvenile fiction. 4. Parent and child – Juvenile fiction.   I. Griffiths, Dean, 1967- . II. Title.
[E] dc23   PZ7.356Ho 2013

Manufactured by Sheck Wah Tong Printing Ltd.
Printed in Hong Kong, China.

Pajama Press Inc.
469 Richmond St E, Toronto Ontario, Canada
www.pajamapress.ca

Distributed in the U.S. by Orca Book Publishers
PO Box 468 Custer, WA, 98240-0468, USA

For the real Hoogie (aka Eryn),
who is now happily in the middle of
everything. And for the rest of the
JETS, with my never-ending love.
　　　–S.M.

To my Holly, whose favorite donut
is the Old Fashioned Plain.
　　–D.G.

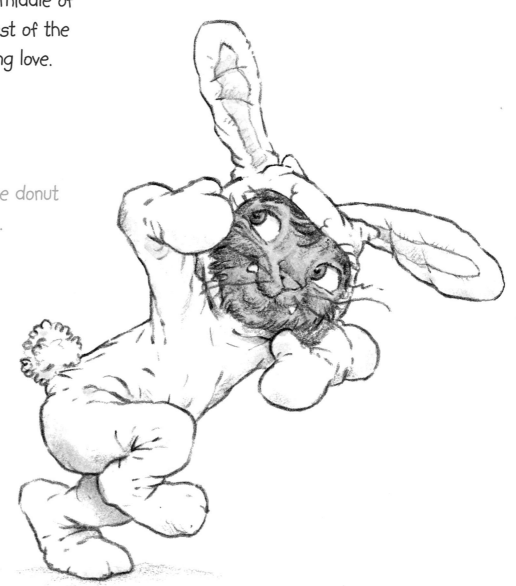

Pumpkin was the first.
Tweezle is the newest.

Hoogie's in the middle.

Pumpkin looks like Mom.
Tweezle looks like Dad.

Hoogie just looks like...Hoogie.

Everyone claps as Pumpkin dances around the room.

They all cheer as Tweezle toddles around the table.

No one sees Hoogie hop.

Pumpkin is the big, big girl you can always count on.

Tweezle is the itty, bitty baby who's oh, so adorable.

Sometimes Hoogie feels like the hole in the middle of a donut.

Pumpkin tells her dream about running with lions.

Everyone gasps...Oh, Pumpkin!

Hoogie explains she had the exact same dream, except it was bunnies.

Everyone laughs...at Hoogie.

Pumpkin's helping Dad
spiff up the wagon.

Hoogie grabs a brush.

"You're too small for this job," says Dad.
"Go see Mom."

Tweezle's drifting off for his nap in Mom's arms.
Hoogie squeezes under Mom's other arm.
"You're too big for this," says Mom. "Go see Dad."

"Too big. Too small.
No room for me at all," Hoogie sighs.

At dinner Tweezle dribbles carrots
and shmushes them in his hair.
Everyone laughs. What a funny, big boy!

Hoogie grabs a fistful of peas.
She squishes and shmushes and makes them fly.
Everyone frowns. Stop being such a baby!

There's a big little pain in Hoogie's tummy.
She feels like the pause in the middle of a giggle.

"Too big. Too small. No room for me at all,"
Hoogie whispers.

After dinner, on the way to the playground,
Pumpkin skips ahead with Dad.
Tweezle toddles slowly with Mom.
Hoogie stops.

"Hurry up, Hoogie," calls Dad.
"You're holding us up,"
says Mom.

Hoogie doesn't move.
The big little pain is getting bigger
by the second, until...

DES!

Pumpkin blinks.

Tweezle hiccups.

"Be a big girl, Pumpkin,
and push Tweezle on the swings,"
says Dad, taking Hoogie's left hand.

"Stay with your sister, Tweezle.
We need a little Hoogie time,"
says Mom, taking Hoogie's right hand.

"You're the sun in the middle of the solar system," says Dad, as they swing her in the air.

"The pearl in the middle of the oyster," says Mom,
as they catch her in their arms.

Hoogie smiles.
She feels like the jelly
in the middle of a sandwich.
Sweet.

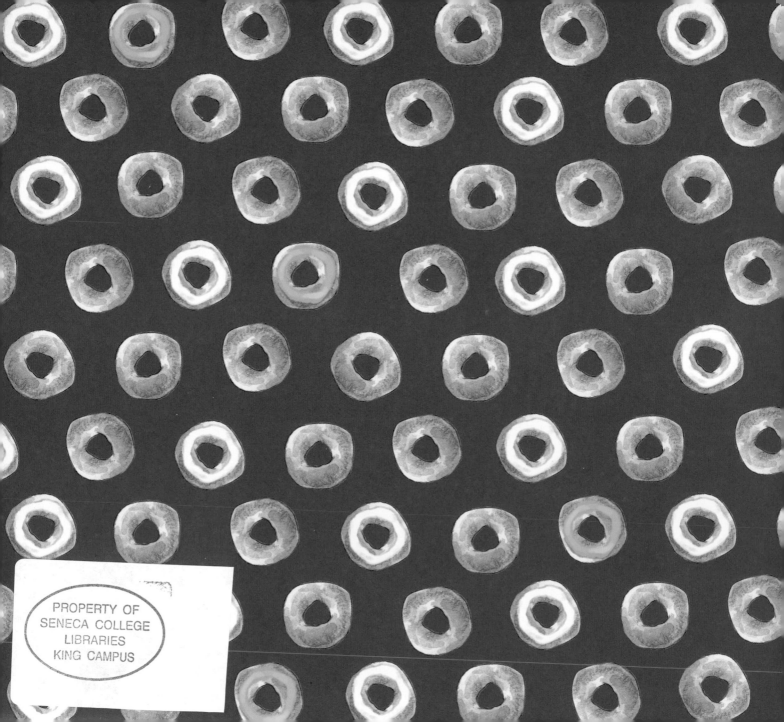